Alma Flor Ada   F. Isabel Campoy

Celebrate
Martin
Luther King, Jr. Day
with Mrs. Park's Class

Illustrated by **Mónica Weiss**
Translated by **Joe Hayes and Sharon Franco**

ALFAGUARA

Mrs. Park's class is getting ready to celebrate
Martin Luther King, Jr. Day.

"Lupe, your drawing of Dr. King turned out really well,"
the teacher says.

"What are we going to put on this part of the mural?"
Nelson asks.

"Here's where we'll write his famous statements:
'I have a dream…'" Jorge recites.

"And here we'll put our dreams," says Jessica.
"But I still don't know what mine will be."

"I know mine," says Rob. "I want Joe to be my friend!"

"Who knows why we celebrate Martin Luther King, Jr. Day?" the teacher asks.

"Because he wanted all of us to be able to go to school together," Rob answers.

4

"And ride on the same buses," Nelson says.

"And everyone to get the same pay for the same work," adds Jessica.

Later, Mrs. Park's class goes out to the garden.

6

As they water the plants they talk to each other:

"We have flowers of every color."

"Yes. They are yellow, red, blue, white…"

7

Then they fertilize the trees and look at them.

"There are all kinds of different leaves!"

"Some are very thin, some are round, others are pointy…"

"Shh, be quiet. Do you see that woodpecker?" says Mrs. Park.

"Look, a sparrow!" Nelson says.

"And here's a hummingbird," says Jessica.

"Our garden is so pretty!" Lupe exclaims.

"That's true," Rob adds. "I think it's because it has so many different colors and shapes."

"Hey!" shouts Jorge. "That reminds me of the things Martin Luther King said! I have an idea…" And he whispers to the teacher.

"That's a great idea!" exclaims Mrs. Park, "but we have to start working on it right away so that it'll be ready for tomorrow."

"Just like the flowers in the garden—of every color!"

"And the trees in the forest—of different sizes!"

"And the birds in the sky—each one different!"

"That's how we all are!"

"Martin Luther King, Jr. dreamed that we would all share the planet…"

"respecting…"

"and appreciating…"

"our differences."

"And he struggled to make everyone understand."

"And now we all have to work together to make his dream come true."

Who Was Martin Luther King, Jr.?

This is Martin Luther King, Jr. Martin was born in Atlanta, in the state of Georgia, on January 15, 1929.

When Martin was a boy, African-American children like him couldn't go to the same school as the other children. At the movies and on buses, African-American people had to sit in separate areas. They couldn't eat in the same restaurants or shop in the same stores as the other people. They weren't allowed to live in the same neighborhoods either, or play in the same parks. This is called "racial segregation."

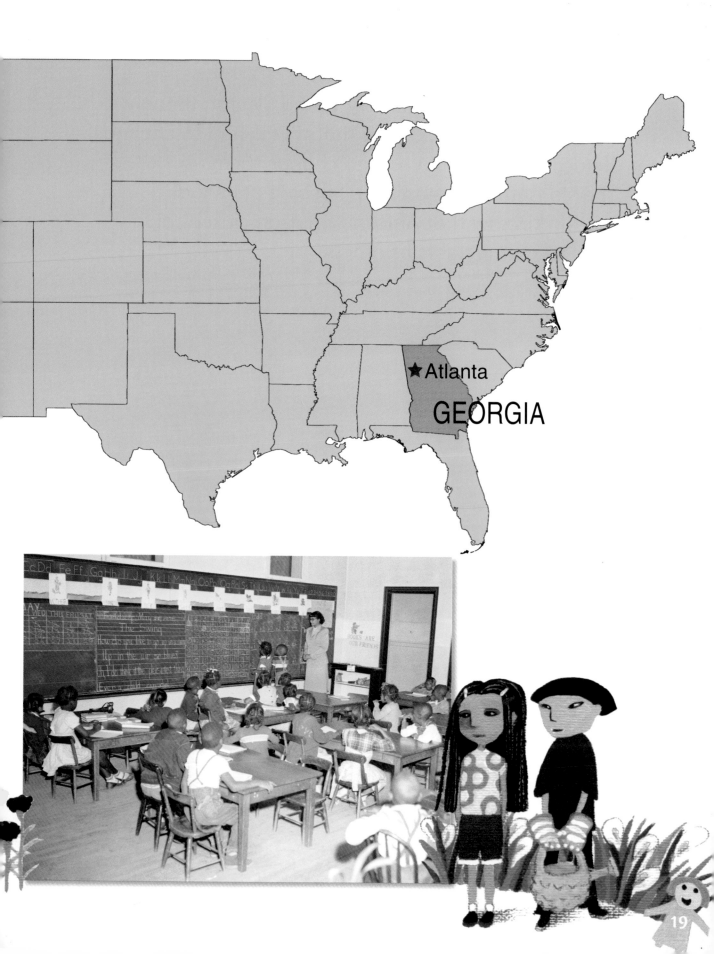

★Atlanta

GEORGIA

From the time he was very young, Martin thought this was unfair. He decided that things had to change. He decided he would help to change them.
The Constitution says that all people are equal.
But Martin saw that African-American citizens didn't have the same rights as others.

Martin traveled all over the country.
He explained to African-American people that it was
a serious problem. He told them not to be afraid to
protest and ask for changes. He encouraged them
to stand up for their rights. But he told them to do
it in a *peaceful* way. He didn't want them to use
violence, insults, or weapons.

African-American people began to march to ask for changes. Martin and his wife, Coretta, marched, too.

One day, an African-American woman named Rosa Parks refused to give up her seat on the bus to a white passenger. Because of this, she was arrested. Then African-American people decided not to ride buses. They did it for 382 days. It was their way of complaining, so that the things would change. They did all this without using violence, following the ideas of Martin Luther King, Jr.

Martin was able to get the support of many white leaders. But many people didn't like what he was doing. They stalked and threatened him. They also threatened his family. They put him in jail about 20 times! But Martin never gave in because he was sure he was doing a very important thing.

Finally, things began to change. In 1956, the Supreme Court ended segregation on buses because it was against the Constitution.

In 1964, President Lyndon Johnson signed the Civil Rights Act. This law ended segregation in schools. It also created programs to help poor people in African-American communities.

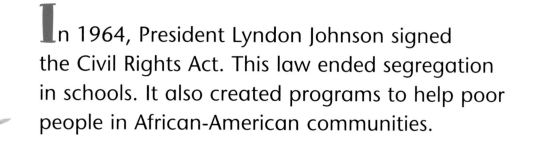

Martin Luther King, Jr. showed that you don't need to use violence to make things change. Martin believed violence doesn't help solve problems. It only creates new problems that could be even bigger and more serious. These ideas made him famous all over the world.

For this reason, he received the Nobel Peace Prize in 1964. It's a very important award that is given to people who work for peace.

Martin Luther King, Jr. is a very important person in the history of the United States. That's why his birthday is a national holiday. Martin Luther King, Jr. Day is celebrated on the third Monday of January with special activities in schools, universities, churches, and public places all over the country.

Martin Luther King, Jr. greets parishioners at the door of Ebenezer Baptist Church, 1964.
© Flip Schulke/CORBIS

Third grade students in a math class at the segregated C.W. Hill School in Atlanta, Georgia, 1954.
© Bettmann/CORBIS

Martin Luther King, Jr. speaks to a crowd in Selma, Alabama, 1965.
© Bettmann/CORBIS

Martin Luther King, Jr. speaks to a crowd in front of the Mississippi State Capitol in Jackson, 1966.
© Flip Schulke/CORBIS

Martin Luther King, Jr. delivering his famous "I have a dream…" speech from the Lincoln Monument in Washington, D.C., August 28, 1963.
© Bettmann/CORBIS

Martin Luther King, Jr. and his wife, Coretta Scott King, lead a group of civil rights activists arriving at the Alabama State Capitol in Montgomery, after 5 days of marching, 1965.
© Bettmann/CORBIS

A group of African-American college students wave to a half-empty bus during the boycott against bus segregation in Tallahassee, Florida, 1956.
© Bettmann/CORBIS

Rosa Parks arriving at a Montgomery, Alabama court, March 29, 1956.
© Bettmann/CORBIS

Martin Luther King, Jr. and other leaders of the Civil Rights Movement celebrate the approval of the Civil Rights Bill in the Senate with senators sympathetic to their cause, 1964.
© Bettmann/CORBIS

Martin Luther King, Jr. in a Jefferson County Court jail cell in Birmingham, Alabama, 1967.
Photo by Wyatt Tee Walker, © Bettmann/CORBIS

Martin Luther King, Jr. and Rev. Glenn Smiley of Texas board a bus together in Montgomery, Alabama, after the Supreme Court ordered an end to bus segregation in that city, December 21, 1956.
© Bettmann/CORBIS

President Lyndon Johnson signs the Civil Rights Act at the White House, July 2, 1964.
© Bettmann/CORBIS

Children at a school in Richmond, Virginia.
© Ariel Skelley/CORBIS

Classmates at a school in the United States.
© JLP/Jose Luis Pelaez/zefa/CORBIS

Martin Luther King, Jr. receives the Nobel Peace Prize in Oslo, Norway, December 10, 1964.
© Bettmann/CORBIS

A street sign on Dr. Martin Luther King, Jr. Boulevard in Harlem, New York.
© Alan Schein Photography/CORBIS

Memorial for Martin Luther King, Jr. in front of Browns Chapel in Selma, Alabama.
© Flip Schulke/CORBIS

Mural in honor of Martin Luther King, Jr. at Martin Luther King Elementary School in Los Angeles, California.
© George Ancona

Celebrate and Grow

Throughout history, and in all parts of the world, people get together to celebrate historic anniversaries, commemorate an important person's life, or to ring in a special period of the year. Common to all these celebrations is the acknowledgment that life is a marvelous gift, and that getting together with family and friends makes us happy.

In a multicultural society like that found in the United States, the fact that so many diverse groups live so closely together invites us to know our own culture better, and to discover the cultures of others. Anyone who explores his or her own culture recognizes his or her own identity in the mirror, and affirms his or her sense of belonging to a group. By learning about different cultures, we can observe life as it appears through the windows of those cultures.

This series offers children the opportunity to get closer to the rich cultural landscape of our communities.

Martin Luther King, Jr. Day

The most wonderful celebration in life is friendship. Our friends are as young as Sebastián, who was just born, and as old as Carmela, who turned 103 in January! Our friends speak different languages; they are artists and athletes, cooks and teachers, and they are from many different backgrounds. They all know how to laugh at a good joke. They have taught us to look in all directions and to learn to respect and admire who they are and the places they come from. Our celebration does not have a specific date, but it does celebrate many heroes, like Martin Luther King, and it means a daily commitment to peace.

Alma Flor Ada and F. Isabel Campoy

To Pablo García Campoy.
And to Collette Lauren, Nicholas Ryan, Jessica Emily,
Cristina Isabel, Victoria Anne, Daniel Antonio, Camilla Rose,
Samantha Rose, and Timothy Paul Zubizarreta, wishing them
the great joy that comes when you start on
the path to peace and justice.

AFA & FIC

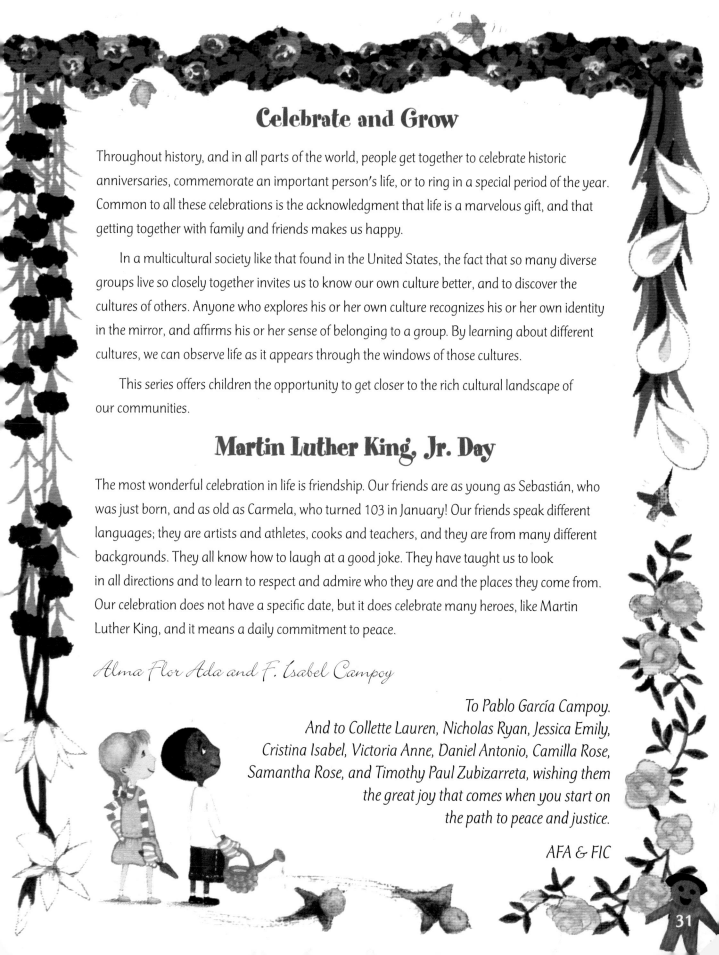

© This edition:
2006, Santillana USA Publishing Company, Inc.
2105 NW 86th Avenue
Miami, FL 33122
www.santillanausa.com

Text © 2006 Alma Flor Ada and F. Isabel Campoy

Managing Editor: Isabel C. Mendoza
Copyeditor: Eileen Robinson
Art Director: Mónica Candelas
Production: Cristina Hiraldo

Alfaguara is part of the **Santillana Group**, with offices in the following countries:
ARGENTINA, BOLIVIA, CHILE, COLOMBIA, COSTA RICA, DOMINICAN REPUBLIC, ECUADOR,
EL SALVADOR, GUATEMALA, MEXICO, PANAMA, PARAGUAY, PERU, PUERTO RICO, SPAIN,
UNITED STATES, URUGUAY, AND VENEZUELA

Celebrate Martin Luther King, Jr. Day with Mrs. Park's Class
ISBN-10: 1-59820-125-5
ISBN-13: 978-1-59820-125-3

Published in the United States of America
Printed in Colombia by D'vinni S.A.

12 11 10 09 08 07   2 3 4 5 6 7

Library of Congress Cataloging-in-Publication Data

Ada, Alma Flor.
    [Celebra el Dia de Martin Luther King, Jr. con la clase de la Sra.
Park. English]
    Celebrate Martin Luther King, Jr. Day with Mrs. Park's class / Alma
Flor Ada, F. Isabel Campoy; illustrated by Monica Weiss; translated by Joe
Hayes and Sharon Franco.
    p. cm. — (Stories to celebrate)
    Summary: The students in Mrs. Park's class prepare to celebrate
Martin Luther King, Jr. Day by thinking about the values he taught. Includes
facts about Martin Luther King, Jr.
    ISBN 1-59820-125-5
    1. Martin Luther King, Jr., Day—Juvenile fiction. 2. King, Martin
Luther, Jr., 1929-1968—Juvenile fiction. [1. Martin Luther King, Jr., Day—
Fiction. 2. King, Martin Luther, Jr., 1929-1968—Fiction. 3. Schools—Fiction. 4.
African Americans—Fiction.] I. Campoy, F. Isabel. II. Weiss, Mónica, 1956- ill.
III. Hayes, Joe. IV. Franco, Sharon, 1946- V. Title. VI. Series.

    PZ7.A1857Celm 2006
    [E]—dc22   2006014839